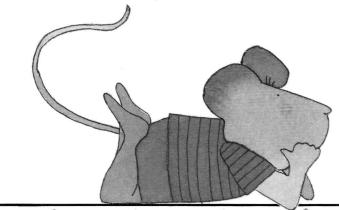

WHAT ALVIN WANTED

by HOLLY KELLER

GREENWILLOW BOOKS, NEW YORK

Watercolor paints and a black pen were used for
the full-color art. The text type is Veljovic.

Library of Congress Cataloging-in-Publication Data
Keller, Holly.
What Alvin wanted / Holly Keller.
p.   cm.
Summary: While baby sitting with their brother Alvin, Libby and
Sam have a hard time guessing what Alvin wants to make him happy.
ISBN 0-688-08933-X.   ISBN 0-688-08934-8 (lib. bdg.)
[1. Babies—Fiction   2. Baby sitters—Fiction.
3. Brothers and sisters—Fiction.]   I. Title.
PZ7.K28132Wg 1990   [E]—dc19   88-34917   CIP   AC

FOR MY GENEROUS FRIEND AVA

Mama hurried to put on her hat and
button her coat.

"I'll be back soon," she told Libby and Sam.

"Take good care of Alvin."

Libby and Sam waved from the
window, and Alvin began to cry.
"What's wrong?" Libby asked. "Mama's
coming back soon."
But Alvin just cried louder.
"Tell us," said Sam. "We know you can."
Alvin shook his head.

"Want a cookie?" Libby asked.

"Or some milk?" said Sam.

"No," Alvin cried. "No, no."

"I know," said Libby. "You want to play a game."

"Hide and seek," Sam said. "I'll be 'It.'"

"No," Alvin cried, and he sat on the floor. "I don't want to play a game."

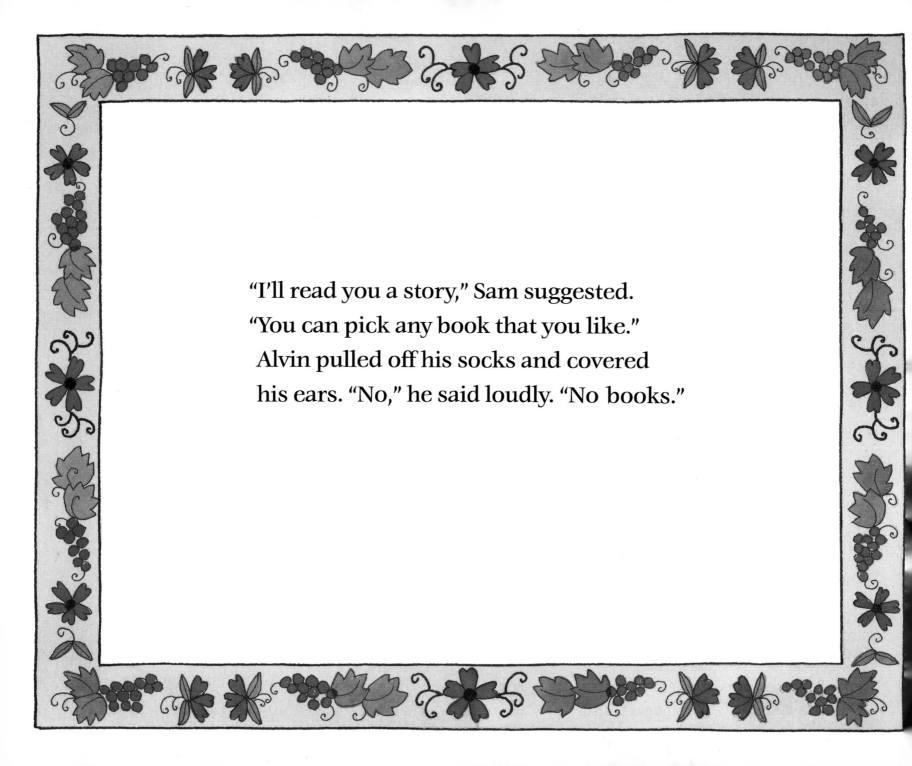

"I'll read you a story," Sam suggested.
"You can pick any book that you like."
Alvin pulled off his socks and covered
his ears. "No," he said loudly. "No books."

"Are you sleepy?" Libby asked. "Would you like to take a nap?"
Alvin sighed and crawled under the table.

Libby got some paper and some crayons from the closet.

"Try to draw us a picture so we'll know."

Alvin made a few scribbles and crumpled them up.

"I can't," he said sadly. "I can't."

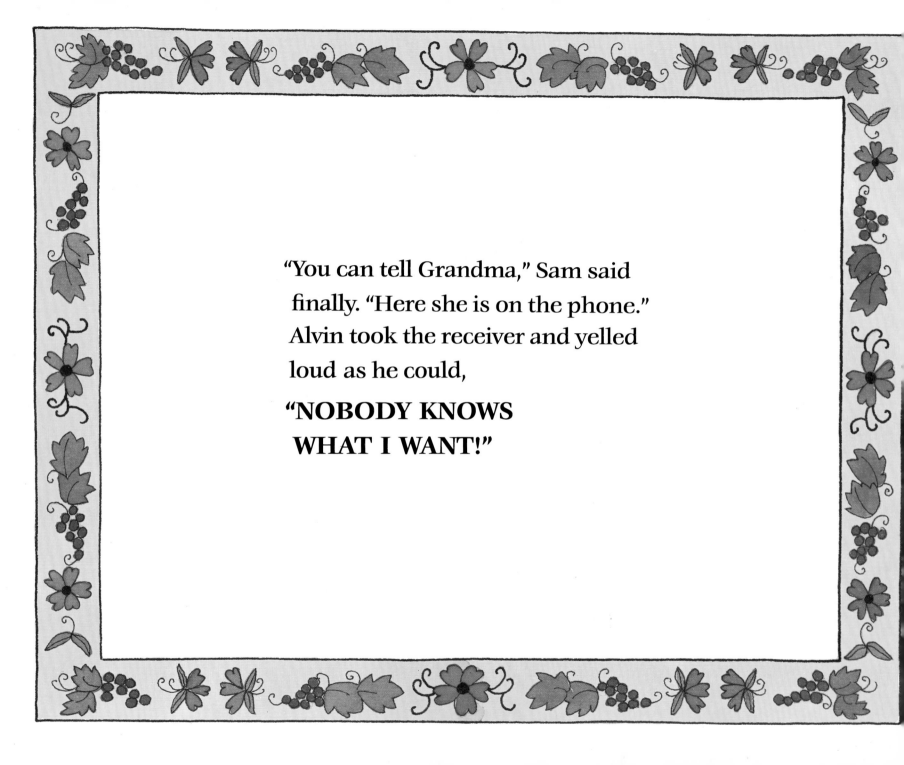

"You can tell Grandma," Sam said
finally. "Here she is on the phone."
Alvin took the receiver and yelled
loud as he could,

**"NOBODY KNOWS
WHAT I WANT!"**

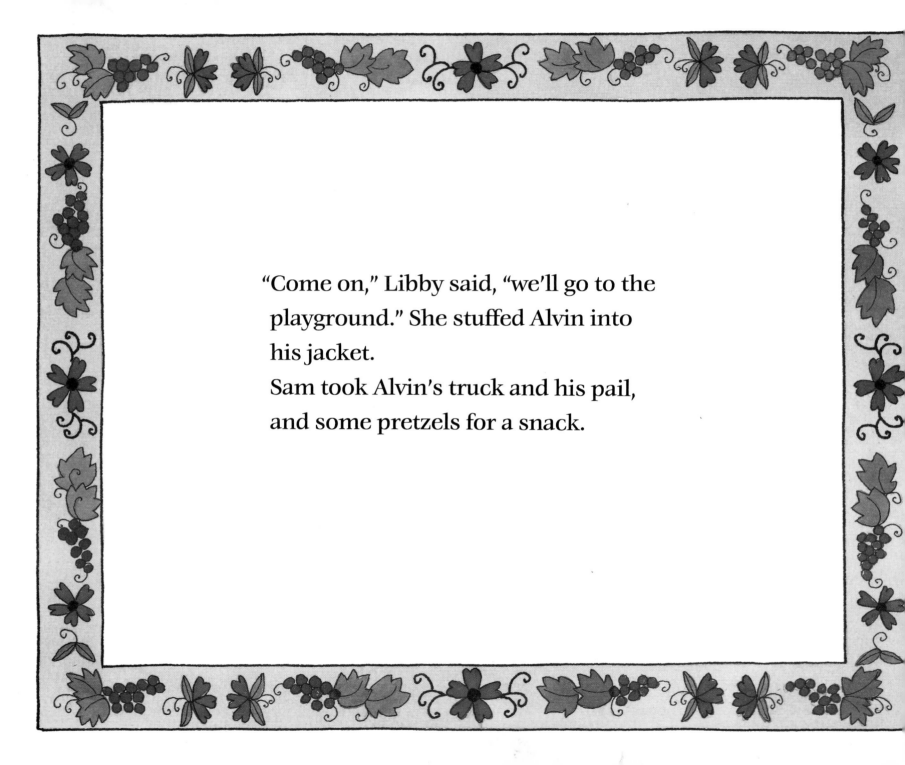

"Come on," Libby said, "we'll go to the
playground." She stuffed Alvin into
his jacket.
Sam took Alvin's truck and his pail,
and some pretzels for a snack.

"The sandbox is muddy," Alvin said
when they got there, "and somebody
is on every swing."
"We'll play with your truck," Sam said,
putting it down, and he made a sound
like a motor.

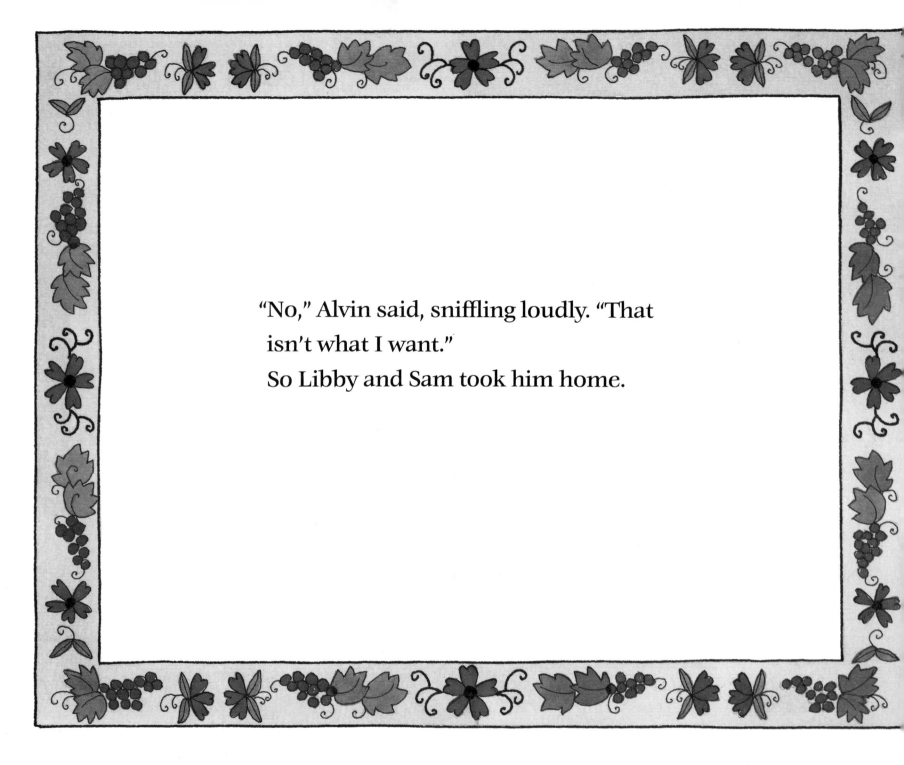

"No," Alvin said, sniffling loudly. "That
isn't what I want."
So Libby and Sam took him home.

"Jeepers," Sam groaned. "Are you sick? Do you hurt? What will make you feel better?"

Just then Alvin heard Mama's key in the door.

"I'm back," she called. "I'm home."

Alvin ran to see her. Libby and
Sam went too.
"Nobody knows what's wrong,"
Libby moaned.
Mama began to smile.
"I know," she said, and she picked
Alvin up. "I forgot to kiss him
good-bye."

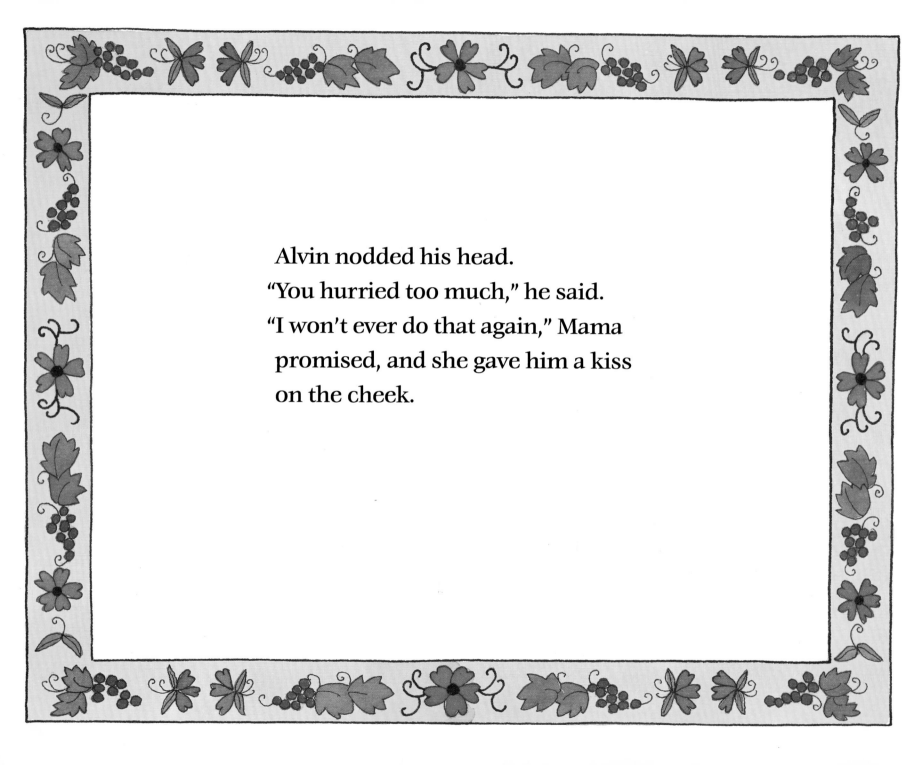

Alvin nodded his head.

"You hurried too much," he said.

"I won't ever do that again," Mama
promised, and she gave him a kiss
on the cheek.

Alvin smiled at last and jumped down
to the floor.

"I'm ready now, Sam. You're 'It.'"